Starfish Bay® Children's Books
An imprint of Starfish Bay Publishing
www.starfishbaypublishing.com

I NEED A PLAN!

© Federica Muià, 2019
ISBN 978-1-76036-059-7
First Published 2019
Printed in China by Beijing Shangtang Print & Packaging Co., Ltd.
11 Tengren Road, Niulanshan Town, Shunyi District, Beijing, China

Federica Muià is an illustrator from the small village of Ivrea in Northern Italy. She studied archaeology and anthropology at the University of Turin, where she participated in various research excavations. Federica has always been curious about everyone and everything. She moved to Cambridge in 2014 to follow her dream of becoming an illustrator and she completed her MA in Children's Book Illustration in 2017. Travelling, drawing, and animals are her passions, which she combines into her stories.

I Need a PLAN!

By Federica Muià

But not for ME.
I CAN'T stay in the sun!

I usually stay out
with my friends and...
it's not FUN!
NOT AT ALL!

I try to test the SUN...

NEVER a good idea!

Experiment
Number 1

Experiment
Number 2

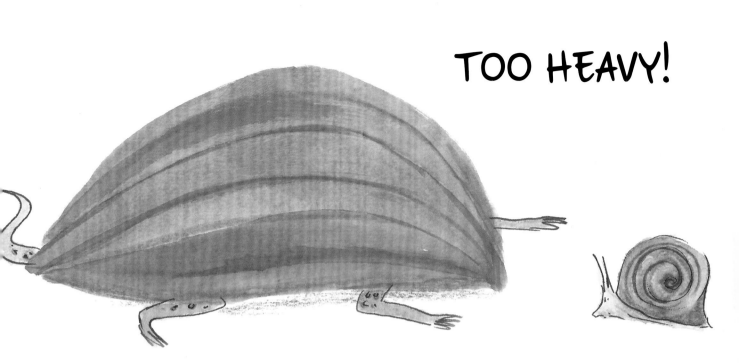

TOO HEAVY!

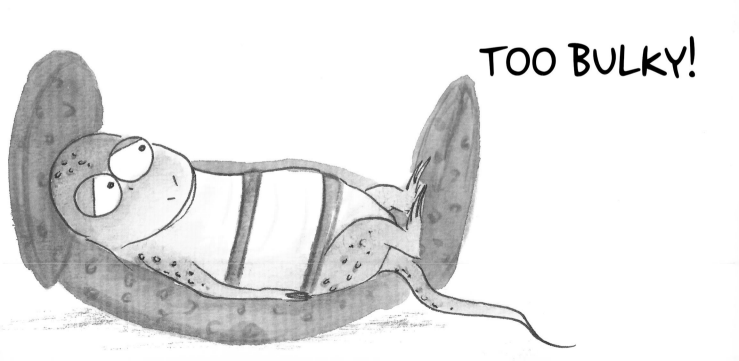

TOO BULKY!

Mmm... yes...
I have an IDEA!

STEP 5
Replan

STEP 6
Redo

Experiment Number 3
SUCCESS!

YES!
This is PERFECT!